King Roger's

King Roger had a sceptre.
King Roger had a throne.
King Roger had a royal crown
And a golden telephone.

King Roger needed nothing
For he owned everything.
The town, the fields, the animals
Were "Property of the King".

Whenever he went riding,
He wore his jacket of fake fur,
His royal watch, his royal crown,
And one golden riding spur.

To keep his crown from falling off
While riding through the land,
He attached it firmly to his head
With a royal rubber band.

But, one day while he was out,
His crown caught on a twig.
His royal crown became detached
From his royal wig.

The rubber band stretched tight,
The twig broke with a crack,
And faster than a royal pigeon
The crown came flying back.

King Roger saw it coming
And smartly chose to duck.
It hit his horse on the head,
The horse, it ran amok.

Across the royal fields it ran,
With King Roger clinging tight,
Followed by a royal servant
And a royal knight.

Royal subjects scattered
As they clattered into town,
Chased by pounding hooves
And a King without a crown.

19

At last, beside the royal moat,
The horse came to a halt,
The King flew up into the air
And did a somersault.

21

Royal servants gasped
As he splashed into the moat.
They helped King Roger out
In his muddy boots and coat.

Now when it's time for riding,
King Roger's properly dressed.
He wears a riding helmet
And a rubber ring around his che